..., Vik...
...ing the seas in the... powerful
...ngships. And in a small village called
Snekkevik, Freya, Wulf and Vik were
born. On the same day!

When Vik lost his parents in a great
battle a year later, he was adopted by
Freya and Wulf's family, who took
him in as their own son.

But Vik and Wulf never did
see eye to eye...

FOR
PER & BODIL

First published in 2008 by Orchard Books
First paperback publication in 2009

ORCHARD BOOKS
338 Euston Road, London NW1 3BH
Orchard Books Australia
Level 17/207 Kent St, Sydney, NSW 2000

ISBN 978 1 84616 727 0

A CIP catalogue record for this book is available from the British Library.

3 5 7 9 10 8 6 4 2

Printed and bound by CPI Group (UK) Ltd, Croydon, CR0 4YY

Orchard Books is a division of Hachette Children's Books,
an Hachette UK company.

www.hachette.co.uk

and the Lucky Stone

Shoo
Rayner

"There's loads of driftwood on the beach," said Vik.

"I'm not going all the way down there," Wulf grumbled.

"C-c-can't we find some wood up here?" Freya shivered. "It's t-too cold to carry driftwood back up those rocks."

Mum had told the children to find some kindling wood for the fire. Winter was drawing in. The dark sky forecast snow, and they needed all the wood they could get.

"Well, I'm going down there…come on, Flek!" Vik and his faithful dog scrambled down the rocks to the beach.

Freya called after them. "We'll go and look for wood in the forest over there."

In no time at all, Vik had collected loads of sticks, which he tied into bundles with long strips of leather.

"Come on, Flek. It's started snowing…let's go!" Vik looked all around him, but Flek had disappeared.

Vik ran down the beach calling Flek's name, but he was nowhere to be seen.

Vik wasn't worried. Flek ran off all the time. *He must have found something tasty to chase*, Vik thought to himself.

"I'm going home, Flek," Vik yelled. "I'm not waiting!"

As he turned to go, Vik spotted something on the ground. A smooth, white stone stood out against the gritty, grey sand. It had shining green and brown stripes on its surface. A perfect hole had been worn through at one end – almost as if it had been made by a jeweller.

Vik tied a leather strip through the hole and hung it around his neck. "It's my lucky stone," he told himself.

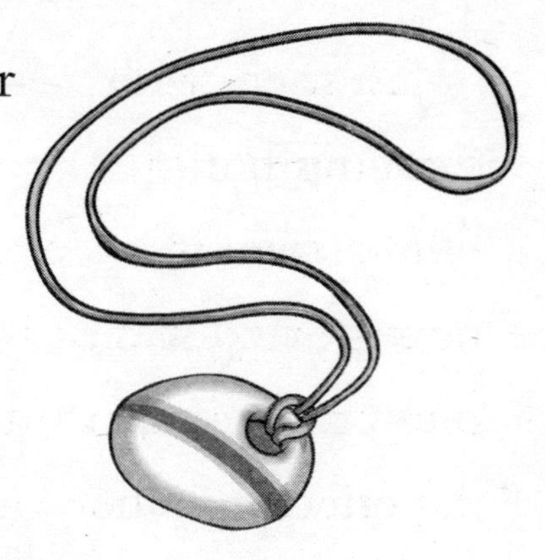

Just then, with a joyous bark, Flek appeared from behind some rocks. He leapt in the air, trying to catch the huge snowflakes that were now falling thick and fast.

VIKING WEATHER

Vikings live in the far, far north. When it snows it really, *really* snows!

The snow can stay on the ground all winter.

Vikings use skis and sleighs to get about on the snow.

Vik picked up his snow-covered bundles and scrambled over the rocks. The wind blew large, white flakes into his eyes.

The ground was already hidden under a layer of fluffy snow. Everything looked different. Vik headed towards the forest.

"Wulf! Freya! Where are you?"

The snow made everything quiet and dampened the sound of his voice. All he could hear was the tramp of his feet and the wind blowing through the trees.

It was late, the sky was dark and the snow was falling heavily. Vik felt very small and very alone. The paths were hidden by the snow and Vik had lost all sense of direction.

"Which way, Flek?"

Flek stared at him. His look seemed to say, "I don't know. You're the leader!"

"The sun sets in the west," Vik explained. "If we head towards the darkest bit of sky, we should get home quite soon. Come on!" Vik didn't believe it, but it made him feel better.

Flek followed. His master was always right, wasn't he?

It was really dark now, and the snow was very deep. Vik was well and truly lost. He pulled his cloak around himself and shivered. "We're going to die," he told Flek. "They'll find us frozen into blocks of ice."

Flek barked and
ran ahead. Vik
strained his eyes.
Was that a light?

As Vik struggled through the snow, the light grew brighter.

"Well done, Flek," he said excitedly. "It's a house!"

HOW NOT TO GET LOST IN THE FOREST

If you are lost in a Viking forest, look at the tree trunks for a natural compass. Moss and lichen like the shade, so they grow best on the north side of the trunks. Now you can work out south, east and west!

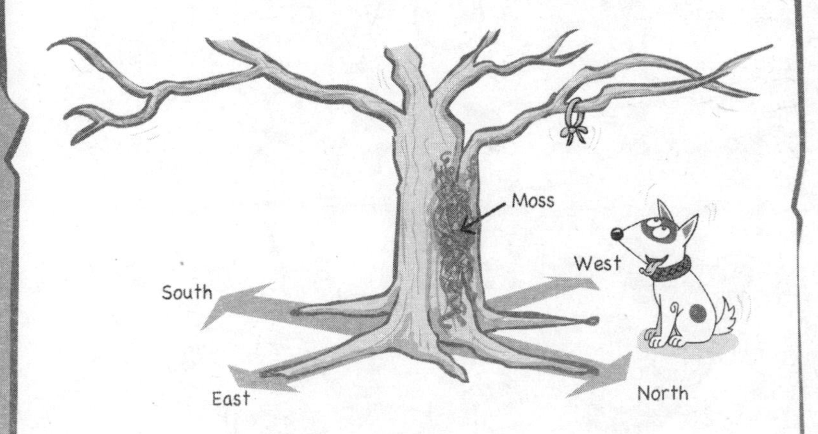

You can also tie red ribbons on the branches to mark your way back.

The door opened a crack. All Vik could see was a pair of suspicious eyes. A thin voice spoke: "Who's there?"

"My name's Vik Haraldson. I'm lost and I'm f-f-freezing to death."

The door opened a little more. An old, bent woman looked Vik up and down.

"I can't leave you out there to freeze, but I don't want any funny business. I've got absolutely no food in the house, so don't expect me to feed you!" she said.

Vik was so pleased to be let into the warm, he didn't care about food.

But once Vik could feel his toes again, his stomach began to rumble, and soon food was all he could think about!

Vik sat by the small fire. He played with his lucky stone and wondered what the great god, Thor, would do...

THOR AND HIS GOATS

Thor's chariot is pulled by two goats. When Thor is hungry, he cooks the goats and eats them.

If Thor wraps the bones up in the skins, he can bring the goats back to life. Now that's fast food!

A cunning plan popped into Vik's head. He winked at Flek before saying, "We could eat my dog!"

"Your dog?" the woman said, startled. Flek tucked his tail between his legs and whimpered.

"Yes," Vik sighed. "Of course, we'd have to use my lucky stone. Dog doesn't taste very nice on its own."

The old woman eyed Vik suspiciously. "How does that work, then?" she asked.

"We need to boil a large pot of water," Vik explained. "We can use the wood I brought to build up the fire."

The woman became quite excited and helped Vik get everything ready.

When the water was boiling, Vik dropped his lucky stone into the pot.

Then he tasted it with a spoon.

"Mmm! Not bad," he declared. "But it would be so much better with an onion."

"Let me see what I've got," said the old woman. She shuffled off and returned with a large onion.

When it had been sliced up and added to the water, Vik tasted it again.

"Mmm! Good!" he smiled. "But it would be so much better with a carrot or two."

The woman tasted it and agreed. "Let me see what I've got," she said.

She was soon back with two large carrots, which she sliced and added to the water.

"Yum!" said Vik. "It's really beginning to taste like something now. But it would be so much better with a handful of beans."

And so the evening went on. Every time Vik tasted the soup, he suggested another ingredient, and the old woman always managed to find what he asked for, even though she had absolutely no food in the house! She even found some salt and pepper.

Soon the lucky stone had magically turned the water into a delicious soup.

SOUP RECIPE

Get a grown-up Viking to help you fry some sliced onions in a casserole dish until they are soft and brown. You could fry some chopped bacon, too.

Add chopped vegetables, beans, salt and pepper, and maybe some herbs.

Add some ham if you like, then a litre of vegetable stock. Cook it long and slow on a low heat.

Don't forget to add your lucky stone for that extra, wonderful flavour. You had better give it a good wash first!

"Now for the dog!" said Vik, picking up a huge knife.

"Oh!" said the old woman, who by now had become quite fond of Flek.

"Of course, dog meat is pretty disgusting," Vik said, "even with a lucky stone. You know, this soup would taste so much better with some ham."

The old woman looked at Flek. Flek stared back at her with his big, brown, trusting eyes.

"Let me see what I've got," she said.

The woman found some ham and a loaf of bread, too. Soon they had filled themselves up with the best meal either could remember eating, and Flek busied himself chewing the ham bone.

"That was wonderful," the old woman said. "And to think it was all made with your lucky stone!"

Vik smiled, snuggled down in front of the fire with Flek and fell into a deep and happy sleep.

They woke the next day to the sound of voices shouting Vik's name. The snow had settled and the sky was clear and blue. Freya and Wulf were searching for him.

"Vik!" Freya laughed when she saw him. "We were worried that you'd frozen to death!"

Vik hugged her. "This kind lady took us in."

"He's a wonderful cook," the old woman said. "He can make a meal out of nothing." Then she explained how Vik had made the tastiest meal even though she had absolutely no food in the house.

As Vik turned to go back home with Freya and Wulf, the old woman held out Vik's lucky stone. It had turned a soupy colour, and didn't shine like it had before.

"You keep it," said Vik. "It's a present to say thank you for saving me last night."

"Thank you!" the old woman exclaimed. "Now I shall never go hungry. Drop by if ever you are passing. I can always make some lucky-stone soup."

"Thanks! I will,"
smiled Vik. "Come
on, Flek...let's go!"

Shoo Rayner

Title	ISBN
Viking Vik and the Wolves	978 1 84616 725 6
Viking Vik and the Big Fight	978 1 84616 731 7
Viking Vik and the Chariot Race	978 1 84616 730 0
Viking Vik and the Trolls	978 1 84616 724 9
Viking Vik and the Bug House	978 1 84616 726 3
Viking Vik and the Lucky Stone	978 1 84616 727 0
Viking Vik and the Longship	978 1 84616 728 7
Viking Vik and the Secret Shield	978 1 84616 729 4